A Paula Wiseman Book • Simon & Schuster Books for Young Readers • New York London Toronto Sydne

Always

Alison McGhee and Pascal Lemaitre

I am the keeper of the castle.

This castle.

And I will keep the castle safe.

I will tame the squirrels.

I will guard against monsters.

I will halt the avalanche.

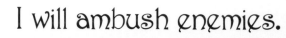

I will ambush enemies.

Always, I will keep the castle safe.

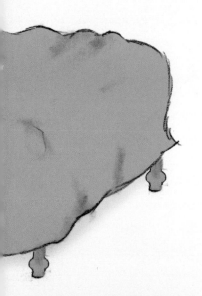

I will protect the blanket.

I will patrol for intruders.

I will stop
savage beasts.

I will chase away evil.

Why?

Because there is nothing I will not do . . .

to keep this castle safe.

I will divert meteors.

I will contain the wind.

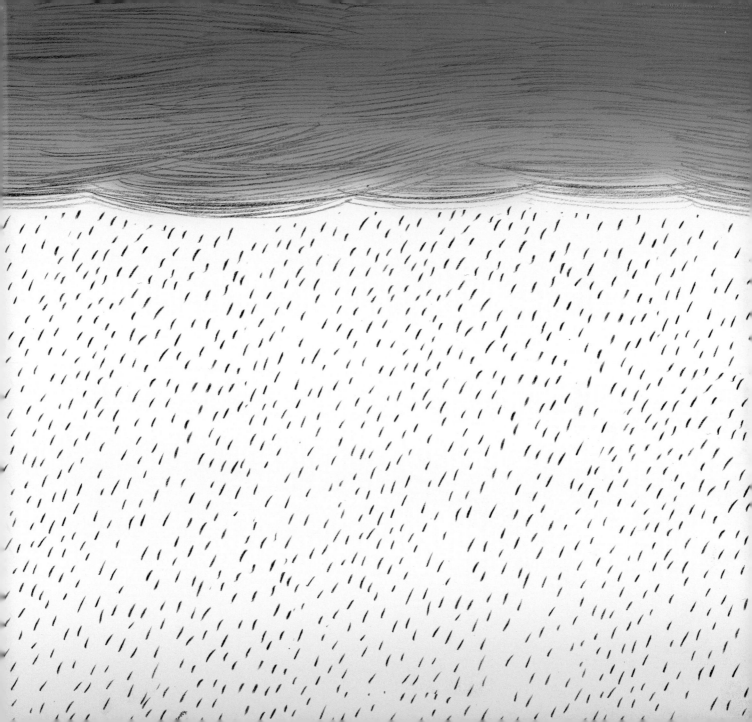

I will calm the sea.

I will keep the castle safe.

Always.

Why, you ask?

Do you mean to say
that you
don't know?

Because
you
live here.

For Wendell, Petey, Moxie, and Kerry and in loving
memory of Lady, Star, Molly Toshiba, and Willis.
—A. M.

For Holly McGhee and Emily Van Beek.
with many thanks to Ann Bobco for her guidance.
—P. L.

SIMON & SCHUSTER BOOKS FOR YOUNG READERS
An imprint of Simon & Schuster Children's Publishing Division
1230 Avenue of the Americas, New York, New York 10020
Text copyright © 2009 by Alison McGhee
Illustrations copyright © 2009 by Pascal Lemaitre
All rights reserved, including the right of reproduction in whole or in part in any form.
SIMON & SCHUSTER BOOKS FOR YOUNG READERS is a trademark of Simon & Schuster, Inc.
Book design by Ann Bobco
The text for this book is set in Harrington.
The illustrations for this book are rendered in pencil, then digitally colored.
Manufactured in China
1 2 3 4 5 6 7 8 9 10
CIP data for this book is available from the Library of Congress.
ISBN: 978-1-4169-7481-9